I'LL BE HOME FOR CHRISTMAS

CHRISTMAS

An Out of Line Novella

JEN MCLAUGHLIN

NEW YORK TIMES BESTSELLING AUTHOR

JEN MCLAUGHLIN

I'LL BE HOME FOR CHRISTMAS

AN OUT OF LINE NOVELLA

Manufactured in the United States of America

Cover Designed by: ProBook Premade Book Covers

Interior Design and Formatting by:

eBook ISBN: 978-0-9907819-6-7

Print ISBN: 978-0-9907819-7-4

✻ Created with Vellum

Out of Line series:

_____

OUT OF LINE

Out of Time
Out of Mind

Out of Line **Novels:**
Fractured Lines
Blurred Lines
I'll Be Home for Christmas

This one goes out to all the Out of Line readers who have been asking me for more. This is for you. Thank you for reading my stories, and wanting more.

ONE

Carrie

———————

$\mathcal{I}$ rolled over in bed, instinctively reaching out for warm skin. I found it and smiled, my eyes still closed. No matter how long we'd been married, or how many times I woke up beside the man I loved with all my heart, I never tired of feeling him there, beside me, every morning.

I never would.

If we'd learned anything from the tragedy that struck our little family a couple of years ago and almost tore it apart, it was that life was too short to take anything for granted. There were no guarantees. Nothing was a given. Not even waking up next to the man you loved.

Not even waking up at all.

The second I touched his skin, he stirred, his eyes

slowly opening. Reaching up, he rubbed his face, skimming over his chiseled jawline and scruffy skin that I love so much. By the time he lowered his hands and finished yawning, his bright blue eyes were on me.

"Morning, Sunshine," he murmured.

I smiled. "Morning."

"Where's...?" He glanced around the room, his eyes going wide. "Wait. Did we actually wake up before Susan and Cory?"

"Mmhm."

"Well, then," he rolled on top of me, cradling his weight on his elbows, but letting his lower half touch mine—and oh, what a lower half it was. "I'm not one to lose an opportunity like that..."

Oh, that's something I knew very well.

Just like I knew him.

We'd enjoyed almost eleven years of marriage and two children. A relationship that started with him secretly guarding me in college, and then me falling in love with him before finding out he'd been lying to me the whole time. Injuries, PTSD, breakups, and gunshots.

So much had happened between us, yet feeling him in between my thighs was as electrifying as the first time he'd laid there.

Perhaps even more so.

His mouth kissed a trail down my neck, wasting no time with sweet kisses or foreplay. When you had an almost eight-year-old and a baby who could wake up any second now, there wasn't time for hesitation or sweetness. You took what you got when you got it.

As often as you could get it.

His fingers skimmed up my thighs, lifting my nightgown as they shifted inward, and leaving a trail of fire in their wake as he bit down on my shoulder just the way I like it. When he touched my core, I gasped and spread my thighs more, letting him have full access to my body.

I was all *his*.

Forever and always.

He cupped my butt and slid under the covers, disappearing. Within seconds, his mouth was on me, and I was burying my fingers in his hair and holding on for dear life because he was about to take me on a ride I'd never forget. I never would.

His tongue rolled over me, stroking me with the perfect amount of pressure to make my heart race, and my legs turn to jelly. I rocked my hips against his mouth, losing myself in him. He held onto me, making sure I didn't go too far as he stroked harder, faster. His fingers teased my entrance, and I came, stars bursting in front of me in beautiful multitudes of red.

He climbed up my body under the covers, dropping love bites the whole way. When he settled over me, he cupped my face, kissed me gently, and then thrust inside me with one hard, full stroke. The contrast of that motion with his soft lips on mine, barely touching me, was enough to make me quiver with need. He buried his face in my neck, moving inside me with sharp, hard movements, each stroke taking me higher and higher until I was gasping his name and scraping my nails down his back.

"I love you, Ginger," he whispered, angling his hips a little more as he drove me to the finish line with a finesse he'd never lost, and only ever improved on.

I tried to tell him I loved him, too, but I couldn't breathe, let alone talk. I gasped, arching my back, closing my eyes as the pleasure took over me, bringing me higher and higher until I was sure I could fly. Finn was right there with me, soaring through the skies as he came, too, my name on his lips like a prayer. We clung to one another as we came down, neither one wanting to be the first to let go. After a few minutes, our hearts calmed, and our breathing evened.

For a minute, I thought maybe he'd fallen back asleep, but then he lifted his head and grinned down at me with the cockiest grin I'd ever seen, which was saying a lot when it came to Finn. "That was one hell of a wakeup."

"Yeah, it was," I said lazily. "But we should get moving soon. She'll be in here any minute now."

"Don't worry, I locked the door last night," he whispered, nibbling on my neck. "We'll have a warning."

As if on cue, the door handle jiggled.

He groaned dramatically and dropped his head on the pillow next to mine.

I giggled.

"Daddy?" Susan called.

"Yeah, baby. I'm here."

"Six more days until Christmas!" she cried, jiggling the handle. "Let me in."

"Daddy's getting dressed," he called out.

"I'm hungry," she said, her pouting about the lock out situation clear even through the door that separated us. "Let's go."

"Okay, go on down. I'll be right there, and we'll start cooking."

It was Saturday morning, which meant Susan and Finn would be making pancakes, sugared strawberries, and homemade whipped cream. There would be coffee for us, and Susan would have hot chocolate with cinnamon in it. She loved that, especially this time of year, with Christmas so close.

"Hurry up, Daddy!" she called.

Her footsteps retreated, and Finn lifted his head again. "Duty calls."

"Yeah, it does," I said, smiling. "Can't say I'm complaining, though. I'm hungry after that wakeup."

He grinned. "Me, too."

With a quick kiss, he pushed off me and headed for our bathroom, barefoot and naked. I enjoyed the view, in no rush to get up. Finn was cooking, so that meant I got to take it easy.

Saturdays were my favorite day of the week.

After a few minutes, he came out, wearing boxers and holding his phone. "Weird."

"What?" I asked, half asleep again.

"Your dad called me."

I frowned. It was still early, only seven. "Did you call him back?"

"Not yet," he said, setting his phone down and stepping into plaid pajama pants. "I will, though." He headed for the door. "Go back to sleep if you want. I'll get Cory if he wakes up, and I'll send Susan to get you when breakfast is ready."

I burrowed into the pillows. "Love you."

"Love you more," he said with a smile, closing the door behind him.

Yep. Saturdays were *definitely* my favorite.

TWO

Finn

––––––––

"*W*ait, slower!" I called out, saving my daughter from pouring the entire container of whipping cream all over the counter. I supported the end, smiling when she managed to get most of it inside the bowl. "There you go. Perfect."

Cory babbled behind us, kicking his feet against the high chair as he shoved a tiny piece of strawberry into his mouth. I smiled at him over my shoulder and flipped the waffle iron. Susan had insisted on Belgian waffles this time instead of pancakes since they were more "Christmas-ey." Christmas music played softly in the background, and the tree shone brightly despite the sunshine streaming in.

If Susan was out of bed, the tree was on.

It was the golden rule in this house.

The front door opened, and I stiffened. Only two people had keys to our home: Carrie's mom, and her dad. They didn't often use them, though, and last I heard, they were in D.C.

So who the hell was coming in *my* house?

I immediately went on guard, tapping Susan on the shoulder. "Stay here, baby, okay? Don't come out unless I tell you. And don't touch the waffle maker, it's hot."

She nodded, stirring the whipped cream with a frown of concentration.

Creeping toward the door, my hand instinctively went to my hip from my days as a bodyguard, but my gun wasn't there. Hadn't been ever since I traded in my security badge and cammies for a computer programming degree. Now I spend my days behind a desk instead of fighting bad guys on the battlefield and off it.

And yet the urge was still there, to reach for it.

Some things never died, I guess.

I crept around the corner, ready to pounce, but Carrie's parents stood in the foyer, shrugging off their winter coats that looked ridiculous here in California. "Mom? Dad?"

They looked at me, smiling wide. We'd gotten off to a rocky start, with them not exactly approving of their rich daughter falling for the help, but over the years we'd gotten close.

Closer than I'd ever imagined possible.

"Surprise!" my father-in-law called out, removing his scarf.

Mom sniffed. "Do I smell pancakes?"

"Waffles," I said distractedly. It wasn't that I wasn't happy to see them, I was, but they weren't supposed to fly in to visit us until Wednesday morning. "Everything okay?"

"Yeah, of course," my mother-in-law said. "Carrie in the kitchen?"

"She's still in bed. Susan and I are cooking."

She brightened. "I'll go see if she needs help while you two talk."

She patted my arm as she passed in a wave of Gucci perfume and high heels clicking on the marble floor. As soon as we were alone, I crossed my arms and squared off with my father-in-law. "What's up?"

"I have a favor to ask of you."

I rested against the wall. "I figured."

"Senator Stapleton and I have a big event on Thursday. It came up last minute after we'd already granted most of our staff holiday time to spend with their families and travel." He sighed, running a hand through his hair. "It's a big deal, and a great publicity opportunity, but I hate to go back on my word with our staff."

Stiffening, I crossed my ankles, too, knowing where this was going, and not liking it. There was nothing I wouldn't do for my father-in-law, but I wasn't comfortable slipping back into the uniform of a security guard. I'd left that life behind me years ago, and whenever I revisited it, bad shit happened. "Dad—"

"I know it's short notice, and I know it's almost Christmas, but we'll still be back in plenty of time for Christmas." He tugged on his tie. "With primaries coming up, we can't afford to miss a chance to get the goodwill of the people at this tree lighting event. Especially with this current political climate."

I snorted. "No one likes anyone right now. I doubt lighting a Christmas tree will change that...no offense intended, of course."

"None was taken, but I intend to change that."

Yes, he did. It was part of his political plan. It was a good one, and he stood a decent chance of winning because of it. But to leave my family this close to Christmas wasn't something I felt comfortable doing. "Where is it?"

"Utah. It's a critical state for us."

I groaned internally. "Mountains or desert?"

"Mountains."

That explained the winter gear. My in-laws came prepared for winter weather. "I don't know if Carrie will go for it."

"Go for what?" she asked from behind me, her voice soft.

"Princess!" her father called, lighting up like he always did when he saw her. "Come here. Give your dad a hug."

Smiling, she came down and hugged him, pulling back to say, "This is a surprise."

"Yeah, I know." He patted her shoulders, making her red curls bounce. "Mom's in the kitchen...cooking."

"God help us all," Carrie muttered, making the sign of the cross. "What were you two talking about?"

"Your dad wants me to travel with him to Utah to help guard him and Senator Stapleton," I said, not bothering to beat around the bush. "Do you mind?"

She frowned. "When?"

"Monday through Thursday," he said, smiling sheepishly. "We'd be back before Christmas Eve dinner, of course. I gave the employees time off before this opportunity came up, and I didn't want to go back on my word."

"Of course not," she said, frowning. She eyed me. "Finn?"

"Yeah?"

"What do you think?" She bit her lip, worrying about me like always. "Will you be okay?"

"It'll be quiet. It's more of a formality than anything." Her dad approached, rubbing the back of his neck. "Stapleton will have his guy, and I'll have mine. You."

"No danger?" she asked slowly.

"I'd be stunned if there was," he answered.

I believed him.

But still...

It had been a while since I'd been in any situations that might spark up my PTSD, and I had no interest in revisiting that world again, but I highly doubted I would have to.

"Are Riley and Noelle coming?" Carrie asked.

"No, they're staying home."

She hesitated, then looked at me. "I'm okay with it if you are."

"Carrie? A little help here?" her mother called out from the kitchen.

Carrie sighed. "I better go."

I kissed her forehead and then she waved off, leaving us alone again. I looked her father in the eye. "No shootouts? No assassins?"

He shook his head. "Absolutely not. There are no threats on my life, yours, or hers. It's just a good publicity opportunity at a few children's hospitals and a fundraiser for natural disaster victims. That's it."

God knows we'd had enough of those this year. "All right, I'll do it, on one condition."

He cocked his head. "Anything."

"Watch the kids tomorrow night so we can go out with some friends before I leave."

His smile widened. "Deal."

We shook on it, and I mentally prepared myself to take a step back in time, to a world where I carried a gun, and protected another person's life with my own who wasn't my wife...

For better or for worse.

THREE

Carrie

———

"*B*ut will he be okay?" Marie asked, her voice low despite the noise all around us. We'd excused ourselves to the restroom, leaving our friends behind. We slowly made our way back to the table now, arm in arm, as I filled her in on my father's odd request to steal my husband away.

"I guess he thinks so," I said, frowning. "Dad says there's no danger, and he promised me there would be no drama. But still, it makes me nervous."

"Me, too," she said, nibbling on her lower lip. "Why not ask Hernandez and Ben? At least they're police officers, and still in the game."

"I guess he wanted to keep it in the family? He trusts Finn. Maybe that's why he went to him? I don't know."

She *hmph*ed.

"How are things with you and Alex?"

Marie frowned. "Over."

"What? Why?"

"He's just not the one." She shrugged, not meeting my eyes. "He bored me."

That's because the one she should be with was Hernandez, but neither one of them would be the first one to admit it. "Maybe that's a sign."

She side-eyed me. "A sign of what?"

"That it's time to stop dating the boring business guys you gravitate toward and try a new type of guy." Marie worked in stocks and trading, and she always went for CEO-types, then tired of them quickly. "Maybe...I don't know. A paramedic, or a firefighter, or...maybe a cop?"

She rolled her eyes. "Real subtle."

"What?" I asked innocently.

We came around the corner and spotted the rest of our party. Noelle had stayed with the boys since she'd just used the restroom, and she spoke animatedly, swinging her arms as she described something. Riley watched her with warmth in his eyes, looking head over heels in love, and Finn leaned back in his chair, smiling with his arm flung over the back of my empty seat. Ben, Hernandez's partner on the police force, listened intently, while Hernandez watched Marie's approach.

Like usual.

The two of them had been playing hard to get since Marie had been my roommate in college, and it was getting a little old. They needed to give it a go already.

"Hernandez looks good tonight," I said, nudging her. "And he's single. He and that blonde that looked like you didn't work out."

"Don't even," she gritted. "Not happening. Never happening."

I rolled my eyes. "Whatever."

We sat in our seats—with Marie as far away from Hernandez as possible—and Finn placed his arm around my shoulders, kissing my temple. "You okay?"

"Yeah." I nodded, forcing a smile. "Of course."

"It'll be okay. I'll be home for Christmas, your dad will make some headway on his campaign, and it'll be fine." He squeezed my arm. "I promise, Ginger."

"I know," I whispered. "I'll miss you, though."

"I'll Facetime you." He leaned closer. "You can give me a little show."

"Only if you give me one, too," I shot back breathlessly, already liking this idea.

He raised a brow. "Demanding."

"Would you have me any other way?"

He laughed. "Hell no. Although, I do also like you naked and quivering on our bed, with my head between your—"

"What's this I hear about you traveling with my dad?" Riley asked, interrupting our little back and forth banter.

I mentally groaned.

Finn winked at me.

Riley and I had been friends for years, and our families had once dreamed of us falling for one another and getting married. We'd tried it, but my heart belonged to Finn. And, eventually, Riley met Noelle, so that door had firmly shut in both sets of parents' heads after that. Riley and Finn were close now, almost as close as him and Hernandez.

"Yeah, Carrie's dad asked me to fill in for security." He shrugged, running his fingers up and down my arm. "It's only a couple of days."

"I was thinking of coming along, too." He glanced at Noelle, who nodded once, then back at Finn. "For fun. Would you mind? I've never been to Utah."

It was so obvious he was concerned for Finn, like me, and I loved him for caring. He was such a good guy. Once upon a time, I'd tried to force myself into loving him because he was just that nice. It hadn't worked, despite my best efforts.

"Of course I wouldn't mind," Finn said, taking his arm off me and reaching for his Coke. "But if you're doing this because you're worried I'll slip, don't be. I'll be fine."

It took a lot of therapy for Finn to be comfortable talking about his issues with others, and I was very proud of how far he'd come. A few years ago, he would never have uttered that sentence. Now that he'd been seeing Doctor Hudson, he was much more open about his past, and his struggle with his addiction to pills and PTSD.

I rested my hand on his knee for support.

He winked at me.

How did he make a wink so frigging sexy?

"No, of course not, man." Riley ruffled his hair. "I just thought it would be fun to get away with you. Have a guy's weekend in between the boring shit our dads are doing." He glanced at Hernandez and Ben. "You guys could come, too. You could fly on my dad's jet with me."

I rolled my eyes. "That sounds like trouble, right there."

"Trouble for all the ladies, maybe," Ben teased.

Hernandez grinned. "You know it."

Marie crossed her arms, remaining silent.

The glower on her face was all that needed to be said, though.

"I'd love to go," Ben said, picking up his beer. "Don't know if Captain would approve of it or not, though. He wants all hands on deck since the Christmas season brings out the criminals even more so than the carolers."

Hernandez winced. "Truth."

"Merry fucking Christmas to us," Ben muttered.

"Word is we might be getting a new Detective soon, too, and there are whispers he might separate us," Hernandez added. "We probably shouldn't give him more of a reason to do so."

Ben deflated. "Probably not."

"All right, it's just us, then." Riley turned back to Finn. "That cool?"

Finn nodded. "Yep."

Noelle reached for me. "We can hang out while they're away. Maybe I'll even stay with you if you don't mind lending out one of your spare rooms. I'll tell you about my latest book, while we drink wine in front of the fireplace after the kids go to bed."

The first real grin of the night broke out on my face. "I'd love that."

"Then it's settled."

I glanced at Marie, who was watching Hernandez. "You want in?"

She broke herself out of her quiet contemplation. "Huh?"

"Noelle is going to crash at my place while the boys are away. Would you like to join?" I asked slowly.

Marie's cheeks went pink. "Uh...yeah. Sure. Sounds fun."

Noelle clapped her hands. "This is going to be epic."

"Yeah, it is," Riley agreed, rubbing her back.

"You know what? Fuck it." Ben pulled his phone out. "We're in. I'll let my dad know."

"Seriously?" Hernandez asked, his tone high with surprise. "You never ask off."

"Well, I am now."

Hernandez did a fist pump. "Fuck yeah. I've never been to Utah. I hear they have some excellent lodges with top-notch craft beers in the mountains."

Finn rolled his eyes. "I'm not helping you pick up chicks, dude."

"I will," Ben promised. He stood, phone on his ear. "If you'll excuse me?"

Marie huffed and sipped her wine.

Hernandez locked eyes on her. "Have something to say?"

"Who, me?" She smiled innocently, her blonde hair falling over her shoulders. "Nah."

"If you say so," he said, smiling just as sweetly.

Finn cleared his throat. "Pack warm clothes. It's going to be cold there."

Ben came back, smiling triumphantly. "Got the approval."

"Yeah!" Hernandez high-fived him.

"This trip just got a hell of a lot more interesting," Finn said, grinning at me.

I laughed. Their excitement was contagious. I lifted my soda, smiling at the love of my life, who looked a lot more excited about this trip than he'd been a few hours ago. "To a very merry Christmas for all?"

Riley held up his beer. "To a very merry Christmas."

We all clinked glasses and drank.

FOUR

Finn

———————

I pressed my mouth to Carrie's, all too
aware of the eyes on us as I said my good-
byes. Her perfect body pressed to mine in all the
right places, something I'd never tire of no matter
how many times I felt it. My tongue teased the
entrance to her mouth, but I didn't slide inside when
she parted her lips for me. Too many eyes on us
for that.

"I love you, Ginger," I whispered.

She clung to me, not letting go as I pulled back.
"I love you more."

"Impossible."

Little hands tugged on my jacket. "Daddy?"

I reluctantly let go of the woman who held my

heart and picked up the little girl who helped her. "Yeah, Pumpkin?"

"Do you have to go?" she asked, staring at me with the same bright blue eyes her mother had. She had a few freckles across her tiny nose, and her mother's hair—but the smile she wasn't showing right now was all me.

"Yeah, I have to help Grandpa do something." I kissed the tip of her nose, then hugged her close, breathing in her strawberry scented shampoo one last time. "But I'll be back in a few days, don't worry."

"Promise?" she asked, her lower lip trembling.

"Pinky swear," I said, offering my pinky to her.

She stared at it, then wrapped her tiny finger around mine.

I kissed her one more time then set her down. Carrie opened her arms for her, and she went to her mother, still staring at me like I'd betrayed her. This shit was hard, man.

If anyone else had asked me to leave my family days before Christmas, I would have told them to go fuck themselves. But this was my father-in-law, and despite our rocky start, he'd been there for me, and helped me climb up from rock bottom. If he needed me, I was there.

No matter how much I wished otherwise.

Forcing a smile, I walked over to Cory, who sat on a blanket by the couch. He was currently happy to remain there, but soon enough he'd be off causing trouble, like usual. The boy rarely sat still, now that he knew how to scoot around on his diapered butt. I knelt beside him and kissed his mostly bald head, ruffling the wispy sandy blond hair. "Hey. Love you, little man."

He grinned up at me, touching my cheek.

My heart broke a little bit.

Standing, I swiped my hands on my dress pants and faced my father-in-law. "Ready?"

He nodded, not quite meeting my eyes. Maybe he sensed how hard this was for me, which made me feel even shittier. The man had done so much for me, and I never wanted to make him feel bad on my account. "Sure, the car's waiting outside with Mom."

I headed for the door, not looking at my family again because if I did, I might not leave them.

When I was halfway out the door, Carrie called, "Wait!"

I turned just in time to catch her. She flung herself into my arms, kissing me with every ounce of love that I felt in my own heart. When she pulled back, she cupped my cheeks and smiled up at me with unshed tears in her bright blue eyes. Her red hair fell around her shoulders, and she wore a black dress that hugged her curves to perfection. "Come back to me."

"Always," I whispered.

We broke apart, and I winked at her. Then I made my way to her father's town car. The door was open and waiting for me. I nodded at the driver. "Hey, Dan."

"Mr. Coram."

I rolled my eyes. "I told you to call me Finn."

"And I told you I could never do so." He winked at me. "But I appreciate the offer, sir."

We used to work together, him and I, before I married the boss's daughter. It was weird how lines appeared when shit like that happened. Guys I used to get drunk with, before I quit booze, were now bowing to me and calling me sir, all because I'd married Carrie.

Fucking ridiculous.

"Tell Sam I said hi."

He bowed to me. "Will do, sir."

I slid into the car next to my in-laws, smiling at them as Dan shut the door. "You guys ready?"

"More than ready," my father-in-law answered. "I'm sorry if I put you in an awkward situation by asking you to attend this event with me. Carrie and the kids could come along, if you'd rather."

Carrie and I had discussed that, but she had

clients booked and didn't want to leave them alone for the holiday season, which was so hard on so many people for many reasons. "It's okay, I'm only going to be gone for a couple of days."

"I know," he said, sighing. "But I felt like I was ripping the two of you apart like the old days, and it didn't feel good."

I laughed, running my hand through my hair. "All due respect, sir, but anytime I have to leave my wife and kids, it's gonna be hard. They're my world."

"I know," he said, smiling.

"It's one of the many reasons we love you," my mother-in-law added, reaching across her husband's lap to touch my hand. "You're devoted to them, and anyone can see that."

I inclined my head, saying nothing.

"I heard Riley and the rest of the boys are coming along," my father-in-law said, rubbing his chin.

"Yeah. Riley kind of turned it into an impromptu boy's trip." I studied him closely. "Is that okay? It won't interfere with my performance, of course."

"I don't mind at all, I love Riley." He hesitated. "And Ben and Hernandez, too, of course."

I knew all too well just how much my father-in-law loved Riley Stapleton. He'd wanted him to marry Carrie for the longest time. I'd wanted to hate Riley. Tried to dislike him on principle for being in love with my wife for years, but the dude was just too damn nice to hate.

Believe me. I'd tried.

"Good." I glanced out the window at my house as we pulled away from the curb, swallowing hard. "Is it snowing in Utah?"

I hadn't seen snow in years.

"A little. There's a big storm coming, but it won't hit until after we leave."

I nodded, watching my home until it disappeared. "Good, because I'm not missing Christmas with my family."

"Neither am I." He tugged on his tie. "Still, it would have been nice if she could have came along. We could have celebrated Christmas in the mountains, with the snow."

A white Christmas. I missed those. Don't get me wrong, I loved California and the life we'd made here. It was my first home, and I'd fallen in love with Carrie on the beaches of my home state. But sometimes, especially this time of year around Christmas, I missed the bitter cold wind whipping through my layers of clothing and my winter hat. The family had a cabin in Big Bear we used to frequent, but after our big fight a few years ago, we hadn't gone back.

I guess we both associated it with bad memories now. I didn't like to think of the time I'd slipped back into bad habits, and almost lost my family. She didn't either.

So we never went back.

"Maybe next year."

The rest of the ride passed in mostly silence, with a few words exchanged here and there. When we pulled up to Long Beach Airport, I scanned the runway for the family jet, but couldn't find it. Sometimes I still couldn't believe that I, the son of a security guard, married into a family who had a fucking private jet. "Where's the plane? Are we early?"

"It had technical difficulties, so we're first classing it today. The Stapleton's and company are joining us. He said if we had to fly commercial, then so did they."

I frowned. "Couldn't we just take their jet?"

"Not big enough."

Sighing, I gripped my knees. I wasn't spoiled, I swear to God. But not having the jet at our disposal when we were flying into snowy terrain made me nervous. What if the snow came sooner? What if the airlines cancelled flights? I didn't like playing with fate—not when it came to my family.

"All right," I said, sliding outside the car when Dan opened the door for me. I turned, waiting for the rest of my family to exit the vehicle when I heard my name called out.

I turned, spotting Hernandez. He wore a winter coat and hat that swallowed up his lean frame. Grinning, I forced my mind off changed plans and tried to relax a little. "You look ridiculous, man."

Hernandez laughed. His dark brown hair showed out of the sides of his winter hat, and his brown eyes flashed with laughter. The dude was always smiling, which was funny, since he used to be one of the most serious guys I knew, back when we were younger. "I know, it's great."

I snorted.

Ben came up behind him, wearing a hoodie and a pair of jeans. I rarely saw him dressed down like that, so it was kind of weird. He held a Starbucks coffee in his hand, and his green eyes were sparkling with mischief. "Hey, man."

We clapped hands and did that man hug thing men did. "Sup?"

"Excited for this vacation. It's been too long."

Hernandez nodded. "*Way* too long."

"Let's get this party started," Riley said from behind me, throwing his arm over my shoulder. He, of course, wore a name brand suit and smelled of expensive cologne. The dude didn't know how to dress down.

Of course, I was in a suit, too, but I was on duty, so...

"Time to check our luggage," my father-in-law said, grinning at all of us.

We nodded and grabbed our shit, heading for the doors. As we approached, Riley held my shoulder, slowing me down. "Carrie okay?"

"Yeah, she's not happy I'm leaving, but she's all right."

"Good. Noelle will keep her busy." He sighed, staring at our group. "She wasn't too happy about me leaving, either, but it'll be good for us. We've been together nonstop, so when I get back, we'll have some wild reunion sex."

I grinned. "Reunion sex *is* pretty amazing."

"You know it, man." He clapped my back. "You know it."

We headed inside the airport with the rest of our group. As we checked in, boarded the plane, took off, and flew over state lines, I couldn't help but think that even though I was on a plane in the sky right now, my heart was firmly back in California.

FIVE

Carrie

———————

"*B*ut did he *really* feel that bad about it?" Marie asked, holding a wine glass between her fingers with her right hand, and a pair of scissors with her left. Since she was right-handed not much was happening as far as her helping me wrap presents went.

The fireplace crackled next to us, occasionally popping with that wonderfully Christmas-like sound. We decided to turn on *Christmas Vacation* in the background, mine and Finn's favorite movie to watch when wrapping presents. Only Finn wasn't here this time.

Marie and Noelle were.

He'd been gone for two days, and he was due to come home Thursday morning. To be honest, I couldn't frigging wait. Two days was too long to be without my man. I loved my friends, don't get me wrong, but I'd fallen asleep in my husband's arms for so long that doing without just felt...wrong. The only other times we'd been apart, really, had been when we fought.

So, this couldn't help but remind me of those times.

It wasn't a good feeling.

Noelle laughed. "No, I don't think he was."

I forced a smile, bringing my mind back to the present. I slapped a piece of tape on Susan's stuffed animal—she loved cats and was obsessed with getting as many of them as possible—before lifting my head. "I don't know, he seemed like he felt pretty bad to me."

Noelle rolled her eyes and set aside a prettily wrapped package for Cory. "Riley's good at looking sorry when he really isn't. That's okay, though. I love him anyway."

"Do you miss him?" I asked.

"Like crazy," she admitted, smiling sheepishly. "But we're kind of used to it. I travel a lot for book signings, and he does the same for his day job. Once he's published, he'll have even more traveling. But when we come back together..."

Marie leaned closer. "Yeah?"

"Reunion sex." She sighed and picked up her wine. "It's the best."

I licked my lips. "Ooohhh."

Marie groaned and set the scissors down. "You guys are killing me. I don't have a guy who's gone, and can give me amazing reunion sex."

"There's an easy fix for that," I said, putting a bow on Susan's cat.

"Don't," Marie groaned. She put down her wine and picked up a board book about dinosaurs for Cory. "This for Finn?"

I rolled my eyes. "Nice."

"Sorry. I'm cranky." She rubbed her forehead and placed the book on the wrapping paper. "I just... I don't know. I don't know why it keeps coming back to him all the time, or why people are trying to push us together. I feel like nothing is working out because people keep putting that thought in my head. If we were going to be together, don't you think it would have happened by now?"

I swallowed. "Well, I mean, have you guys ever...you know...?"

"No, God, no." She cut the wrapping paper, her blonde head lowered. "We kissed, once, in college, and then he started acting all possessive over me, so I was like, no way."

Frowning, I thought back. "Did he?"

"Yep."

Noelle sighed. "He was pretty young back then, though. Maybe he's changed?"

"He's definitely changed," I agreed. "He used to be one of the most serious people I knew. Never smiled. Only spoke when spoken to. But then over the years, after he got out of the military, he changed. He's funny and talkative, lighthearted..."

Marie rolled her eyes. "Maybe you should date him, then."

"I would if I didn't already have the love of my life by my side," I shot back. "Don't you want that, too?"

"You know I do," Marie muttered. She lowered her head again. "He just...I don't know. He intimidates me. The way he looks at me, it's like if I let him, he would consume me."

Noelle smiled. "Riley looked at me like that, too, and it scared me."

"Finn, too," I said slowly, remembering the heat in his eyes after our first kiss all those years ago. He still looked at me like that. Like he couldn't live without me. "Notice a trend here?"

Marie shook her head. "I don't know if I can do it."

I said nothing, not wanting to press her more. Naturally, I wanted my best friend to be happy, and in my opinion, she could find that happiness in Hernandez. But if she wasn't ready?

She wasn't ready.

Noelle handed me the wrapped present, then reached for another from Cory's pile. "How did you know Finn was the one, Carrie?"

I picked up the Fingerling Monkey Finn had scored for Susan. "We had a rocky start, as you know. When I fell for him, I fell hard, but he kept pushing me away. When we finally got together, he...well, to steal Marie's words, he consumed me. He was my world. I thought I finally understood what love was, and why people were willing to do anything for it."

Noelle nodded, eyes on me. "Mmhm."

"I was there. She's telling the truth." Marie picked up another present. "He was all she thought about. All she talked about. At the time it was annoying, but it was also inspiring."

Noelle nodded, all wrapping forgotten as the scissors dangled from her fingers.

"But then I found out that he worked for my dad and was protecting me for cash, so I called it off with him. Even when he begged me to give him a chance, even when he told me it had always been more than just a job between us, I didn't believe him. I couldn't bring myself to hope again, because it crushed me, thinking I'd been nothing more than an assignment."

Marie shook her head. "All you had to do was look at that boy to see it wasn't."

"I know, but back then..." I shrugged. "Anyway, after we split, I felt like half of me was missing. A while after that, I got sick, and he found me. He carried me to his place, and took care of me despite his own issues with vomit—something he still has to this day."

Noelle shuddered, touching her stomach. "Me too."

"I guess that's when I knew. I loved Finn, and despite everything, I was ready to forgive him, so...I did. I might not have said it right away, but that was the moment I knew for me, it would always be him. At the time, I'd been trying to make it work with Riley—"

Noelle straightened. "That was then?"

"Yeah."

Marie snickered. "Awkward."

"Not at all, he told me about it." She laughed. "He also told me he was in love with you for years, despite respecting and caring for you and Finn. He just couldn't shake it."

I blushed.

Marie chimed in with, "Yeah, he was, but he never looked at her like he looks at you."

"How did you know Riley was the one?" I asked,

trying to take the focus off my failed attempt to fall for her husband. I picked up my wine and took a chug.

"He asked me to marry him when I was going down on him."

I choked on my wine, coughing and gasping for air.

Marie cracked up, holding her stomach and laughing so hard tears streamed down her face. I hadn't seen her lose it like that in...well, years. "Are you serious?" she finally managed to ask.

"Dead," Noelle said, grinning, getting back to wrapping. "From then on, I knew he was the one."

"Because he asked you to marry him..."

"When his dick was in my mouth," Noelle finished for me. "Yep."

Marie laughed again. "Why, though? Why then?"

"Because it was so spontaneous and fun."

I lifted my brows. "That doesn't sound like Riley."

"I know, which makes it even more real now that I know him." Noelle taped the wrapping paper. "When he was with me, he was a different guy, and maybe on some level, I recognized that in him, even though I didn't know it at the time."

Marie stared at Noelle, her lips parted.

"Then when I, too, found out that we weren't going to work out after all, on that awful night..." She swallowed hard. "It broke me."

I reached out and squeezed her knee. I'd been there that night, and it had been terrible to see them fight like they had. Riley had been cold, a different man, and he'd almost lost her because of that.

Marie cleared her throat. "Luckily, he came to his senses, and now we have you."

"And I have you guys," she said, smiling at us both.

I blinked rapidly. "I love you guys."

"Take the wine away," Marie joked. "She's drunk-loving on us."

"I'm not drunk," I argued. I wasn't. "I haven't gotten drunk since college."

Having a husband who couldn't drink without slipping back into his bad habits kind of made it hard. We usually didn't even have alcohol in the house, despite his ability to not touch it. I didn't like to make it harder on the man I loved to stay clean, thank you very much.

Marie frowned. "How's Finn been?"

"Fine. Perfect. Finn."

Noelle hesitated. "He was hooked on pills?"

"Yeah, after his injury overseas back when I was in college...he almost died. And when he was recovering my parents found out about us, his dad died...it was bad. Really bad."

I looked away from her, not liking to revisit that time in my life.

Marie grabbed my hand, this time. "They broke up, her and Riley hung out, he thought they were hooking up, and they kind of relived history. After the attack on Riley and Carrie, where he saved them—"

"Oh my God, you were with him then?" Noelle cried.

"Yeah. He didn't tell you?"

"No. I mean, kind of." She hesitated. "When we talked about it, I didn't know you yet, but he told me he was with a friend who was attacked for ransom with him." She licked her lips. "It never occurred to me that friend was you, but it makes sense, considering your fathers' connection."

"Yeah."

Noelle waved a hand. "Go on. Continue."

"Oh, right. Well, he got clean with help, and then he came back into my life, but we didn't get together right away. He'd said some awful things to me when we broke up...but when he saved me again, it all just kind of poured out, and we got back together. He went to college with my dad's help, so did I. We got married, and all was good until a little after Susan was born. He got in an accident, and acquired pain pills without me knowing..."

"Enough of this," Marie interjected. "He slipped up, they made up, now they're happy."

Noelle nodded. "Yeah, let's move on." She looked at the present she was wrapping. "Your kids are adorable."

"Speaking of which... You guys thinking of having kids anytime soon?" I asked.

"We..." She cleared her throat. "We're trying. We were pregnant a couple of months ago, but we lost the baby, so..."

"Oh my God, I'm so sorry." I dropped the present I was wrapping and crawled over to her, hugging her. Marie did the same. "I had no idea."

"We didn't tell anyone," she said, holding onto Marie and me.

"I lost a baby, too, when I was shot."

Noelle nodded. "Riley told me about that."

"We're so depressing, guys," Marie said, sniffling. "It's Christmas. We're supposed to be fricking jolly. Ho ho ho, and all that crap."

We all laughed, hugging each other closer. As we held one another, I realized that no matter how much I missed my husband, I was a lucky girl because I had friends like them.

That was never anything to take for granted.

SIX

Finn

—————

*W*e sat at the glitzy hotel bar, everyone a few beers in while I nursed my coke. Riley's words were slurring a little bit, and Ben was a goner. Hernandez had only had one, so we were having fun laughing at the drunk assholes. Riley didn't usually drink around me, but Ben had insisted on having a drinking partner tonight, and Riley had drawn the short straw.

I'd never seen Riley this wasted before.

It was fucking hilarious.

"But then I said, listen here, woman, I'm the man, and I make the rules."

I cracked up. "No, you didn't."

"You're right, I didn't," he said, grinning. "I told

Noelle I'd do whatever made her happy because I loved her, and then we fucked."

I laughed, tossing my head back. "Yep. That's marriage for ya."

"Truth," he agreed.

Hernandez rolled his eyes. "You guys are ridiculous."

"You're just jealous because you can't do it," Riley said, pointing at him.

"Jealous of being married to the same boring woman my whole life?" He snorted. "Yeah, no thank you."

"Neither of us is marrying anyone anytime soon," Ben agreed.

They high-fived each other.

I rolled my eyes. "Whatever."

"Have you ever been in love?" Riley asked, slurring his words.

"Who? Me?" Hernandez asked.

"Both of you, but you first."

Hernandez sighed. "Nope. Never bit that bullet."

"Why not?"

"Never met a girl who made me forget logic," he said dryly. "Love is the biggest weakness a guy can have. I'm not against it or anything, but I have yet to meet someone who makes me want to become weaker instead of stronger."

I shook my head. "Being in love makes you stronger, not weaker."

"If she loves you back, sure."

Riley squinted at him. "This is about Marie."

"Jesus, not everything is about Marie," Hernandez snapped. He looked at Ben. "Your turn to answer the question."

Ben blinked. "What question?"

"Have you ever been in love?" Riley repeated, letting go of the whole Marie thing.

Ben opened his mouth, shut it, and opened it again. "Once, yes."

"Tell us," Riley demanded.

Ben sighed. "We were in high school, and I loved her with all my heart. We were going to go to school together, marry each other, have kids...but then one day, she up and decides to leave town and me. She never came back. Went to college at Duke instead."

Riley whistled through his teeth. "Why?"

"I have no idea, to this day." Ben shrugged. "Probably never will, since I have no intention of ever talking to her again. Even if she did come back to Somerton."

Hernandez grimaced. "Let's hope that never happens. I'd never hear the end of it." He made a face and mimicked his partner. "'Sarah said this, and then Sarah did that, and she's so mean.'"

"Fuck you," Ben shot back. But he ruined the angry words by laughing.

Hernandez winked at him. "In your dreams, pal."

Riley snorted.

"Did you ever love anyone before Carrie?" Ben asked me.

I shook my head. "It's always been her."

"We all saw that," Riley said.

Ben focused on Riley. "You?"

"Carrie," Riley admitted.

"Wait, seriously?" Ben asked, straightening.

"Dead," I said dryly.

"And you two are still friends?"

Hernandez crossed his leg over his knee. "Why wouldn't they be?"

Riley nodded at me once.

"Yeah, why wouldn't we be?" I echoed.

Ben blinked, saying nothing.

My phone vibrated in my pocket, and I pulled it out. Carrie was Facetiming me. I held it up for the guys. "Speaking of Carrie..."

"Answer it," Riley said, grinning. "I might get to see my Noelle."

I swiped the screen, grinning when Carrie's face popped up. Her cheeks were pink, and she was very smiley, so I suspected she and the girls had hit the wine tonight. I always felt guilty that she didn't drink much because of me, but she assured me she didn't give a damn. "Hey, Ginger."

She smiled wider. "Hey yourself. What are you up to?"

"Hanging with the boys." I panned the phone around, showing her everyone, and they all waved at her. "You?"

"The girls." She did the same, showing me the mess our living room was in. Presents, wrapping paper, scissors, and tape covered the Mahogany wood floor. "We're wrapping presents."

I lifted a brow. "I see that."

"Show me my wife," Riley called out.

I rolled my eyes, but when Carrie handed the phone to Noelle, I did the same with Riley. He lit up when he saw her, and immediately stood up and walked off with my phone.

"Unbelievable." I gritted my teeth. "He stole my Facetime."

Hernandez laughed. "Yep."

The waiter came, and we all ordered coffee. It was time for two of us to sober up. We had our big tree lighting ceremony tomorrow afternoon, then it was back home the next morning.

I couldn't fucking wait. I missed my wife.

Riley came back and handed me my phone. When I glanced at it, I wasn't sure what or who would be on the other end, but it was my wife. She'd left the living room, and was climbing the stairs. I grinned at her. "Whatcha doing?"

"Heading to our room. The girls went on a pizza run."

I frowned. "They're sober enough?"

"They Ubered it."

I relaxed. "Good."

"Can you excuse yourself?"

I glanced at my buddies. "Yeah..."

"Then do it." She went into our bedroom, flicked the light on, and bit her lip. "You owe me a naughty Facetime session, you know."

My dick instantly hardened, and I glanced around to make sure no one heard her. Of course no one had. They were too busy ribbing one another to listen to our conversation. "I'll be right back, guys."

They all nodded, not really paying attention to me.

Even if they had heard her, I still would've gone.

I made my way to my room. As I entered the elevator, she laid on the bed, holding the phone over her face. Her red hair cascaded all around her like a halo, and I wished more than anything that I was there with her, so I could touch the silken strands.

She licked her lips and trailed her fingers down her shoulder. "Are you alone?"

Biting my tongue, I nodded.

Lifting the phone a little more, she touched her breast, lowering her hand over her stomach, and down between her legs. "I miss you, Finn."

"I miss you, too," I managed to croak.

The doors opened, and I hurried through them and down the hallway to the left, reaching my room in record time. As I entered, I turned the lights on and locked the door.

She moved her fingers over herself, moaning. "Hurry up, I've got a head start."

I kicked my shoes off and stumbled toward the bed, undoing my pants as I went. "You're so damn hot, Ginger. It won't take me long to catch up."

"Good," she whispered breathlessly. She slid her skirt up, showing me her black panties. Her manicured finger worked over the satin, in slow, big circles. She was teasing herself, not ready to go over the edge yet. If she wanted to come, she'd be moving faster with shorter circles.

We both knew that made her come faster.

Groaning, I closed my fist over myself, watching her as I pumped my shaft. She bit her lip, quietening a moan, and demanded, "Let me see. I want to see you."

I lifted the phone higher as requested, watching her fingers as I jerked off and pretended it was her touching me instead of myself. "I want to taste you, Ginger. So fucking bad."

"You are," she breathed. "Right now..." She closed her eyes for a second. "I can feel you."

My cock hardened even more, and my heart sped up because her fingers moved faster, harder, and I was right there with her. Two nights without my girl were two nights too many.

She cried out, arching her back. As I watched her come, I gritted my teeth as I jerked faster and harder until I joined her in bliss, tilting my head and pumping my hips one last time. Moaning, I dropped back to the mattress, breathing heavily. She did the same.

"That was fucking hot," I said, smiling.

She nodded, closing her eyes. "Yeah, it was."

"And needed," I said gruffly.

Carrie opened her eyes. "*Very.*"

I lifted my head, squinting at the clock. "Shit, it's eleven?"

"Yep. Hence why they left to get the pizza instead of delivery." She rolled over onto her stomach, lifting her legs in the air behind her. She looked sexy as hell, all mussed and flushed. "Do you miss me?"

"More than words can express."

She pouted. "Same."

"Tomorrow's the last night."

"It can't end soon enough," she said, still pouting. She turned her head, then faced me again with wide eyes. "Crap, they're back. That was fast."

I grinned. "That's what she said."

"Ugh," she said, rolling her eyes—but there was no hiding the grin teasing her beautiful lips, or the sparkle of amusement in those baby blues. "I have to go before they realize what we did."

"Shit, I'd tell them. Brag about it."

She gasped. "No."

I laughed. "Fine. But I will."

"Don't you dare!" she gasped again. "I could never look them in the eye again if they knew I booty called you."

Women were so weird. "We're married."

"I *know*." She pointed at me. "Don't tell them."

"Fine, I won't tell them." I grinned. "Now go have fun, I'll see you soon."

She stared at her screen, biting on her lower lip. "You look so hot right now."

"Back atcha." My cock came to life again because she was looking at me like she wanted to go for round two. "Love you, Ginger."

"Love you, too."

We clicked off, and I cleaned myself up, washed my hands, then returned to my friend's downstairs. As I approached, they watched me, and Ben's eyes widened. "You look like you just got laid."

I snorted. "I was in my hotel room alone."

"With your wife," Hernandez pointed out.

"Did you just Fucktime?" Ben asked incredulously.

I laughed. "Is that a thing?"

"Yes, it's a thing," Hernandez said, rolling his eyes. "And you totally just did it."

"I don't know what you're talking about," I said, keeping my word about not telling them what I'd just done since Carrie seemed to care. "I just went to my room to talk to my wife."

"Yeah, sure," Hernandez said.

"And I'm the pope," Ben interjected.

I grinned. "Pleased to meet you."

Riley stood. "I'll be right back."

He practically ran off.

We watched him go, and then all laughed at the same time. As we joked about Riley's eagerness to get his wife on the phone, my mind was a few hundred miles away in California.

One more night...

And I'd be home.

SEVEN

Carrie

My heels clicked on the marble floor as I passed store after store, not finding what I was looking for in any of them. Although, in all reality, how did one find what they were looking for when they didn't know *what* they were looking for in the first place? Buying gifts for Finn was hard because he was the type of guy who didn't ask for much. He was happy with a kiss or a hug. He just didn't put much stock in gifts of any sort.

My phone buzzed, and I pulled it out of my purse. Marie and Noelle were watching the kids so I could shop, so I expected it to be one of them. I was pleasantly proved wrong.

It was my husband instead. *Hey, Ginger.*

Hey, babe. How's the tree lighting going?

Boring as hell. We're at lunch now, then heading back out.

I grinned and typed back fast. *What time does the jet leave tomorrow?*

We didn't take a jet, we flew first class this time.

I frowned. *Why?*

Something about mechanical issues.

I passed Bath and Body Works, its fragrance practically punching me in the face. *Okay, then when does your flight leave?*

11:30. Can't wait to see you and the kids again.

Smiling, I paused in front of Victoria's Secret. *Me either.*

It's freezing here. How's it there?

Warm and sunny, like usual. No snow?

Not a lot. Just enough to have fun in.

I sat on the bench outside Victoria's Secret. Even a few stores away from it, I could still smell Bath and Body Works. Maybe I should get some fruity "grown-up" body wash for Susan, and a little body pouf. She'd love that. *Good.*

All right. Break's over. I'll talk to you soon.

I sighed. *Love you.*

Love you more.

Lifting my head, I checked out the lingerie in the window. It was black, with lace in all the right places, and sheer fabric everywhere else. I bit my tongue, picturing the look on Finn's face if he saw me wearing that. He'd pull me in his arms, and kiss me until I couldn't breathe. Then he'd back me against the wall, pooling the fabric in his hands as he lifted it up my body, inch by inch...yeah, I think I found present number one.

Heading inside the store, I browsed the risqué collections and ended up leaving with the lingerie from the window and a few pairs of sexy panties. After all, a girl could never have too many panties. Sighing, I held onto my bag and headed for Bath and Body Works, idly glancing at the television in the restaurant on my left. It was talking about a big storm sweeping across the country, and I stiffened when I saw how close to Utah it was.

Don't stress, he'll be home.

He promised me...and Finn never broke a promise.

Forcing my mind off the storm I almost passed the perfect gift for him. I stopped in my tracks, backing up a couple of steps to check out the pocket watch in the window. Finn's father had always carried a pocket watch, and Finn had used it until it died a few years ago. Even now, he carried it with him sometimes for good luck, even though it no longer told time.

Maybe it was time for a new one.

Smiling, I headed into the store, feeling lighter than I'd been moments before. I'd found the perfect gift for Finn, and I knew just the way to give it to him.

As I walked out of the store, watch in tow, I almost ran into someone. I reared back, immediately ready to apologize, but the words died in my throat. "Noelle? What are you doing here?"

"It occurred to me I needed to do some last-minute shopping, too. So when Cory went down for his nap, I left Marie in charge." Her gaze fell down to the bag in my hand, and she grinned. "Finn's going to love whatever's in that bag, isn't he?"

I smiled back. "God, I hope so."

"I'm sure he will." She nodded at her own bag. "I had the same idea."

Laughing, I pushed my hair out of my face. "The one in the window suckered me in."

"Oh my God, me too." She pointed. "The black one?"

My cheeks heated. "Yep."

"Guess our guys have similar tastes," Noelle joked.

"Or we do."

She laughed. "True!"

We fell into stride together. "Looking for anything else?"

"Not really. Just kind of window shopping. You?"

I pointed at Bath and Body Works. "I was thinking of getting Susan some goodies from here. Want to join me?"

"Sure," she said, smiling.

Noelle was a newer addition to our group, as her and Riley had only been married for a year or so, but over the past year I'd learned a lot about her. Her parents had been criminals, so when she hooked up with Riley not knowing he was the son of a politician —one who hoped to one day soon be in the White House—things had looked bleak.

She and Riley had even split for a while.

But then they'd come to their senses, and Noelle had been a part of our lives ever since. I was happy about that. Despite not getting much alone time together until this week, we'd clicked immediately, and she had a big heart.

"Oooh, look at this one," she said, holding up a cupcake scent. "She'd love this."

I took it, nodding. "Perfect." I sniffed it. "Ooh, it smells good."

"Strawberries!" Noelle cried triumphantly,

holding it up like she'd found the hidden clue to curing the common cold. "And peony!"

I cracked up. "You're way too excited about this."

"I used to always want to buy stuff here as a kid, but we never had the money," she admitted, tucking her hair behind her ear. "It's still weird, having it. I feel like I take it for granted sometimes, you know?"

"I do know." I picked up all three of the scents and headed toward the body poufs. "I mean, I always had money, growing up, but I think it's too easy to forget how much people struggle sometimes, you know?"

She nodded. "I do."

"Every Christmas I have Susan pick out a family to sponsor from the giving tree at church. I take her out and she shops for them, and I remind her how important it is to give back. It's something I've always taken seriously, since I was old enough to understand just how lucky I was to be born into the family I was."

Noelle touched a lotion. "What did you used to do to give back?"

"Soup kitchens." I gave her a half smile. "Finn would get so mad at me if I went there alone in college, because it wasn't in the best section of town, but I refused to stop. I still go once a month to help out. I also volunteer at the abused woman's shelter, too."

Noelle's eyes widened. "Wow. That's awesome."

"What do you do?"

She hesitated. "I sponsor a couple of children in Africa. Donate to Red Cross. Pretty much anything I see that catches my eye and my heart. SPCA. All those commercials get me..."

"Oh my God, me too."

"If Riley wasn't allergic, I would have adopted all the cats by now," she said, spreading her hands out in a sweeping gesture—and almost knocking over a display.

I laughed. "*All* the cats?"

"Every last one."

I picked up a pink pouf. "I want a cat but Finn keeps saying no. I want one of those smooshy faced ones that have no nose."

"Persians," she said.

"Yep."

"They're adorable. I had one growing up. She would snort when she got excited."

I laughed. "That's the best thing I've ever heard."

"Right?" She pursed her lips. "I wonder just how allergic Riley is..."

Shaking my head, I walked up to the register and paid. As we walked out, the weather was on the television again. I stopped in front of it, gesturing at the screen. They were talking about timelines of the storm. The weather men had moved it up from tomorrow night to tomorrow morning, as it had picked up speed. My heart sank, and I stopped dead in my tracks. "Did you see this?"

"See what?" she asked, frowning.

"The weather. A bad storm is heading for Utah, and it's ahead of schedule." I adjusted the bags in my hands, staring at the screen as people pushed past us, annoyed we were in the way.

"Crap," she muttered. "Want to grab a drink so we can listen in before heading back? Cory's asleep, and Marie was painting Susan's nails when I left."

I hesitated, but then nodded. "Yeah, let's sit at the bar area and see what we hear."

"I'm sure it's fine," she said, her tone uncertain.

We sat down, and the second my butt hit the stool, my phone rang. Noelle's did, too. We looked at one another, eyes wide.

"It's Finn," I said.

"Riley," she returned.

"Both of them, at the same time." My heart twisted, and I said, "I have a bad feeling about this."

She swallowed hard. "Me too. If we don't answer, they can't tell us what we don't want to hear, right?"

"Right..."

We locked eyes, sighed in unison, and swiped our screens. Slowly, I held my phone to my ear. "Hey, babe."

"Don't panic," he said immediately. "I know you're probably watching the news, and thinking the worst, but don't do it. Flights are being cancelled, yes, but ours is good."

I closed my eyes. "So you'll be home for Christmas?"

"I'll be home for Christmas, Ginger."

EIGHT

Finn

———————

"This is a fucking mess," I muttered to Hernandez.

He gritted his teeth as an old man with white hair and a Ralph Lauren polo bumped into him. The man shot Hernandez a dirty look for getting in his way, even though he hadn't moved in five minutes. Ignoring him, Hernandez said, "You're telling me."

We stood at the airport with our luggage surrounding us. Hordes of people pushed by us, each more annoyed than the one before because flights were being cancelled left and right. People were stranded for the holidays, moods were low, and everyone looked two seconds from punching the person blocking their path to possible freedom.

I'd never missed the private jet more so than I did now.

Our flight wasn't due out till eleven in the morning, but my father-in-law and Riley's father decided to show up to the airport the night before because they were hoping to get a different flight out. As of now, they had not succeeded because all the flights were booked up, cancelled, or overbooked. Big shocker there.

I paced back and forth, holding my third coffee of the night. It was only three in the morning, which meant we had another eight hours of hell to go. "Where's Riley and Ben?"

Hernandez tipped his head. "Over there."

Riley was passed out with his head on Ben's shoulder...and Ben was equally passed out with a baseball cap pulled low over his eyes. I grinned and chuckled. "Now, that's just perfect."

"I may have Snapchatted it to them both using the elf filter on them."

I laughed even more.

It was a miracle I could even laugh right now, but if anyone could make it happen, it was Hernandez. He'd known me for longer than anyone else in my life...minus Carrie's parents.

They didn't count, though.

"We're getting home, man. One way or another."

I rubbed my forehead. "I know, but I just wish we weren't dealing with this shit in the first place. If we'd just scheduled the flight last night, or taken our jet..."

"I know." Hernandez clapped me on the shoulder. "It'll all work out, though."

I dropped my hand. "I can't miss Christmas with my family. If I have to walk barefoot through the snow—"

"—both ways, uphill—"

I flipped him off. "Fuck you. I'll do it."

"I know you will," he said, laughing. "Because you'd do anything for your family."

Nodding, I glanced at my father-in-law, who was making his way toward me. His tie was still perfectly in place with his suit jacket buttoned up. I'd undone mine ages ago, and my jacket had gotten shoved into my carry on. My tenure as a security guard was almost over, and then it was back to reality. Thank God. I didn't miss this life. Didn't miss constantly being on guard...

Although, in all honesty, I was always on guard, anyway.

It just wasn't my job anymore.

I liked the life of a computer programmer. No one shot at me or my wife. No one threatened us. All I did was sit behind a desk for eight hours, hit the gym on my way home, and go back to my family by six p.m. It was the perfect life. Life with Carrie was perfect.

Jesus, I was fucking ridiculous.

Pining away for my girl like a teenager.

I wouldn't have it any other way, though.

"Finn?" my father-in-law asked.

I faced him with a calm expression. It wasn't his fault we were in this mess, and I wasn't about to take my frustration out on the man who had been like a father to me ever since mine had died. "Yeah?"

"Are you okay?" he asked, rubbing his jaw.

"Yeah, I'm fine."

"We're getting on that plane, one way or another." He flexed his jaw. "I'm not willing to miss Christmas with them any more than you are."

I nodded. "Glad we're in agreement."

The attendant behind the desk picked up the microphone and cleared her throat. "I know a lot of you are here early for Flight 2206 to Long Beach, California, so I'm going to make this announcement here, as well as putting the information up on the board. Your flight is not cancelled, but it is being moved up to seven a.m. We are hoping by doing this, we will get out before the storm hits, and get you to your families. Please stay tuned for any changes in schedule, plans, or flights. Thank you, and have a wonderful flight."

Mr. Wallington smiled. "See? God is on our side."

"Yeah. Totally," I said, forcing an optimism to my voice I didn't feel. "Storm's supposed to hit at six, though, so I'm not sure that's going to be early enough."

My phone buzzed, and I glanced at it. Carrie's smiling face flashed on the screen. "That's Carrie."

"Take it," he said, patting my back. "Tell her we'll see her soon."

I forced a smile. "Will do."

Excusing myself with a nod, I headed to a quiet corner of the terminal. When I'd talked to her last night, she'd seemed to be in high spirits still, but I knew my girl. She was probably in full blown panic mode by now. I might be there, too, but I wouldn't let her see it. The second I lost my shit in front of her would be the second she knew things were in jeopardy, and I wouldn't worry her like that. Even if I was drowning and about to die, I wouldn't let her see me panic.

She didn't need that in a man. She needed me to be strong.

"Hey, Ginger," I said, smiling even though she couldn't see me because I swear to God she could tell when I was faking it if I didn't. "Shouldn't you be asleep?"

She scoffed. "As if."

"What's up?" I asked lightly.

"They moved your flight up?"

I let out a laugh. "Stalking the site?"

"Of course," she said, her voice tight. "I can't sleep until I know you're on your way home to me."

I rubbed the spot between my eyebrows. "What did I tell you?"

"That you'll be home for Christmas, but—"

"No *buts*." I gripped my phone. "Nothing, not rain, snow, storms, bombs, accidents, or acts of nature can keep me from getting home to you, Carrie. I'm coming home."

I heard her take a deep breath. I could picture her sitting in our bed, her eyes closed and her lips parted on a sigh. It was like I was with her, in that bed, and this was all just a nightmare I'd dreamed up in the middle of the night. "Okay."

"I love you, and I'll see you soon." I hesitated. "I promise."

"I love you, too."

Turning back to my group, I watched as Hernandez sat and stretched out, yawning long and wide. He looked seconds from falling asleep, and I wished I could join him, but I wouldn't be. If something went south, and our flight got cancelled, we needed a plan B.

I had to be awake to make one.

"Get some sleep, Ginger. I plan on keeping you up late tomorrow night."

She let out a low laugh. "Is that another promise?"

"You know it."

I could practically hear her smile through the other end of the phone. "I look forward to collecting on that."

"I look forward to delivering on that."

NINE

Carrie

The sound of the bedroom door flying open and slamming against the wall brought me into consciousness abruptly, and I sat up, gasping, my hand on my chest. For a second, just a *second*, I'd magically travelled back to that awful time when some crazy dude shot me in my own foyer and I almost died. It took me a while to come out of that huge hole, and I had no intention of ever crawling back into its darkness again.

I stared at the intruder, confused at first because it wasn't a child like I'd expected. It took me a minute to focus on the face of the person gesturing wildly at me, pale and wide eyed. My heart pounded so hard from the scare that it took me a second to focus on the actual words coming out of her mouth. "Get up!" Noelle cried, tears running down her face.

Blinking, I tossed the covers back and threw my legs over the side of the bed. "What's wrong?"

"Didn't you see it?" she cried, obviously too distraught to remember she'd woken me up from a dead slumber.

"See what?" I asked gently, crossing the room to place a hand on her shoulder.

She shrugged me off. "The plane. There was an accident—"

My heart dropped to my stomach. "*No.*"

"It tried to take off in the snow, but slid off the runway, and crashed into another plane. It...they..." She covered her face, choking on a sob. "There were deaths, unconfirmed amounts."

My throat closed up, and I staggered back. Without a word, I raced to my phone, picking it up. It took me three tries to unlock it, and another three to call Finn. I trembled so badly I almost dropped it as it rang, and rang, and rang...without an answer.

Eyes wide, I hung up and immediately tried again. With each ring of the phone, I tried to reassure myself he was fine. It was fine. Everything was fine.

Ring.

He's not hurt.

Ring.

He's not dead.

Ring.

He's okay.

Ring.

He's just unable to answer.

Ring.

He promised he'd be home.

Ring.

He never broke his promises.

Voicemail.

I listened to his voice, tears streaming unchecked down my cheeks. When it beeped, I managed to speak. "Finn. Tell me you're okay. Call me. I need you to...I need you."

Hanging up, I looked at Noelle. She was as much of a wreck as I was, and also held her phone to her ear. "Riley, don't you dare do this to me like he did. Don't you *dare*. Call me."

It was then that I remembered her past, and the fact that she'd lost her husband on her wedding night. He'd been hit by a drunk driver. Seeing the hollow look in her eyes as she hung up and called him again hit me hard, and I swallowed past my own fear.

She needed me. Needed reassurance.

I made my way over to her, pulling her into my arms. She held the phone to her ear, letting it ring, as

I smoothed my hand down her hair, trying to comfort her...and myself.

"Shh. It's okay. They're fine."

Riley's voice picked up on the other line, but it was only his voicemail.

She hung up and started calling him again, but I took the phone out of her hand and set it down. She tried to grab for it again, but I pushed her hand away. "Leave it. What if he's trying to call?"

"He's got to be okay." She rested her head on my shoulder, sniffing. "They need to be okay, Carrie."

I nodded, tears rolling down my cheeks. "I know."

"Look, I know it's Christmas Eve and all, but isn't it too early for—?" Marie came in, yawning, half asleep. She took one look at us and woke up instantly. "What's going on?"

"The plane. There was an accident."

She paled, not moving. "Have they called?"

"No, and they're not answering."

She covered her mouth, eyes wide. "Were they all on the plane?"

"Y-Yes, I think so," I said, swallowing hard and hugging Noelle closer as she sobbed. I was as devastated as her, but it was kind of my job to take care of people. I couldn't turn off the fact that Noelle needed a person to lean on right now, and that person was going to be me.

But *Finn.*

Marie snapped out of it and rushed toward us, pulling us both into her arms. "Guys, they're fine. I'm sure they just can't turn their phones on yet, or something. Or they got lost..."

I closed my eyes.

Noelle sniffed and pushed back, eyeing me. "I'm sorry, Carrie. I'm sure you're even more upset than me. He's the father of your children..."

I shook my head. "That doesn't make me more upset than you. I'm sure we're both the same...but we have to have faith they're okay. If Finn was gone...I'd know it in here." I touched my chest. "He's not gone."

She sucked in a breath. "I don't feel it, either. Last time..."

"Did you feel it?" Marie asked.

"I did." She swallowed and pushed her dampened hair off her cheeks. "But I don't now."

"Me either."

Marie nodded. "They're fine. I'm sure of it."

"Try calling your dad," Noelle suggested. "I'll try my father-in-law."

"And I'll try Hernandez," Marie added, bolting out of the room.

I walked toward my phone while Noelle grabbed hers.

"Carrie?" Noelle said, her voice thick.

Facing her, I calmed my features. "Yeah?"

"Thank you. I'm sorry for falling apart on you like that."

I shook my head and picked up my phone. "There's nothing to be sorry for."

She inclined her head at me.

We both dialed.

Ring.

Please answer.

Ring.

Be okay.

Ring.

Come home.

Ring.

ANSWER.

It wasn't until the voicemail picked up and I heard Finn's voice that I realized I'd called the wrong number. I was supposed to be calling my father. I closed my eyes and listened to his voice anyway. I'd been next to him when he recorded this message, and if I listened closely enough, I could hear Susan giggling in the background as she tried to snatch his phone out of his hand so he couldn't play on it, since she had been waiting for him to read to her.

Tears burned, but I blinked them back.

After the phone beeped, I hung up. This time, I called the proper number, but was greeted with the same outcome. Voicemail—this time, my father's. I listened to his warm, professional tone, then swallowed hard at the beep. "Dad, it's me. Call me as soon as you get this."

Hanging up, I took a second to compose myself before facing Noelle. We locked eyes, and both shook our heads. I opened up Finn's location on my iPhone and let out a breath.

Nothing.

"No one is answering," Noelle whispered.

I frowned down at my screen that wouldn't show me where my husband was. "Think of it this way. If they're all not answering, maybe it's a good sign. Like, you know, what are the chances they were all hurt? The plane was still on the ground when it crashed. It can't be that bad, right?"

Marie came in with a purpose, remote in her hand. I wasn't even sure where she'd gotten it from, or when she'd picked it up. She flipped the TV on. Within seconds, she flipped it to CNN, but they were talking about the President's visit to Africa, not the plane crash. "Come on," she muttered, shaking the remote as if that would fix it.

The screen flashed, and it changed to the plane

crash. I moved closer, staring at the fire on the screen with horror as the newscaster spoke. "Tragedy struck in Utah, when a plane took off in icy conditions, slamming into each other. Reports say the plane skidded out of control. The sound of screeching tires and scraping metal could be heard from inside the airport. There are preliminary confirmed casualties of at least twenty, but we are waiting for updates from the police as to whether that is an accurate number or not."

I sank to the bed, staring at the screen with my heart thudding against my ribs.

Noelle sagged against the wall, tears streaming down her cheeks.

Marie stood in shock, staring at the TV.

"Mommy?" a tiny, all too familiar voice said.

Marie jerked, turning the TV off.

I stood up, smoothing my hands over my cheeks, and let out a long breath. By the time I turned around, I was as calm as I could hope to be under these circumstances. "Hey, baby. You're up early."

She rubbed her eyes and came toward me. Holding her favorite stuffed cat by the tail in her left hand, she yawned. "I heard voices. Is Daddy home yet?"

"N-No. Not yet. It's just us," I said, forcing a smile. "You hungry?"

She nodded, pouting. "I want Daddy to come home and feed me. I want to wait for him."

My heart twisted. What if... what if he never got to do that again?

What if he didn't come home?

My breath got stuck in my chest, and I started heaving, trying to breathe.

"Mommy?" Susan asked, her little face crumbling. "Are you okay?"

"I'm...I'm fine," I gasped, faking a cough. "I just..."

Marie must've noticed how close I was to losing it, because she rushed forward and grabbed Susan, pulling her into a tight hug in her arms. "Can I make you eggs? I make the best eggs ever."

Susan smiled up at her. "Okay. I like eggs."

Marie walked off with my daughter, and I covered my face, taking a shuddering breath. I couldn't lose it in front of my kids. Not now. Not *ever*. I rested my forehead on the wall, closing my eyes and counting in my head. One. Two. Three. *Finn was fine.* Four. Five. Six. *He wouldn't leave me like that.* Seven. Eight. Nine. *We were going to grow old together, and rock in our rocking chairs with grandkids on our laps and the sunsets at our backs.* Ten.

He promised me he'd be home for Christmas.

TEN

Carrie

———————

*T*he next hour passed ridiculously slow. It was filled with constant phone checks, a lot of CNN web browsing since I didn't want the kids to see the crashed airplane on TV. Susan ate three helping of Marie's eggs, which she tried to get me and Noelle to eat, but we both just pushed them around on our plates and thanked her for the delicious breakfast.

Our coffees went equally untouched.

Susan was now in the living room watching some show about mermaids living on earth and hiding their true identity, but for the life of me I couldn't remember the name of it. Marie sat beside her, braiding her hair, and Noelle stared straight ahead without blinking. She'd gotten dressed, and every time there was a noise at the door, she jerked and jumped to her feet.

No one was ever there.

I unlocked my phone for the millionth time, checking for any updates or messages. Still no more news on the plane. Still no texts from my husband. Still *nothing*.

Aggravated, I tossed the phone onto the couch, glancing down at Cory as he scooted on his butt to my feet and touched my leg. "Hey, buddy."

He smiled up at me, completely oblivious to the pain piercing through me, and tugged on my pants. As I bent down to pick him up, two things happened simultaneously.

One: Noelle's phone rang.

And two: The front door opened.

We all froze, staring at one another.

"Is it—?" I started.

"It's him!" she cried, lurching to her feet.

I stood, too, staring at my own phone, willing it to ring.

It wasn't until Susan stood up, taking off for the door and yelling "Daddy!" that I remembered the door had opened, too. I'd told her Daddy was coming home today before she went to sleep last night, so it was no surprise she assumed it would be him.

Don't get your hopes up.

Trembling, I slowly followed her. My heart thudded double my footsteps pace. As I rounded the corner, I stopped mid-step, my eyes glued to the man I loved. He held Susan in a bear hug, swinging her in his arms and laughing as she squealed in delight. He stood in the doorway, the smile on his face easily the most beautiful thing I've ever seen in my life, and I couldn't look away.

He was so wrapped up in Susan that he didn't even see me.

"Hey, Pumpkin! I told you I'd be home soon."

She pulled back and cupped his cheeks with her tiny hands, like he always did to her. "I missed you."

"I missed you, too." He kissed her nose. "And your mom and brother. Where are they?" H scanned the foyer, landing on me, and his smile brightened. "There she is." He started my way, grinning, and whispered to Susan. "Mommy's turn for some kisses."

I choked on a sob, covering my mouth.

He stopped dead in his tracks, his jaw dropping. "Why are you crying—?"

Marie hurried in and practically dragged Susan off Finn's chest kicking and screaming, as he stared at me like he'd seen a ghost. Funny, I felt the same way.

After we were alone, he took a step toward me,

his face ashen. "What's wrong? Did something happen? Is Cory okay?"

"Cory is fine," I bit off, torn between screaming at him for not calling me and being so frigging grateful he was here and alive that I didn't dare to be angry. "Everyone is fine, apparently."

He blinked. "Are you angry with me?"

"Why didn't you call me back?"

"I didn't know you called me," he said slowly. "Our phones were off for the flight, and I was so excited to get here that I just got in the car and waited to see you in person to let you know I was coming home early."

I choked on another sob, and took off running for him, hitting his chest. "You stupid, *stupid* man."

"I—" He jumped in surprise, catching my arms and blinking at me. "What the hell—?"

I sobbed and threw myself into his arms, hugging him so tight that I hurt my arms.

"Carrie, baby." He smoothed my hair back, hugging me. "Are you okay? What the hell is happening right now?"

I buried my face in his chest and breathed in tight. "I thought you were *dead.*"

"Dead?" His forehead wrinkled. "What? Why?"

Riley came in behind him, holding his phone. "Apparently our original plane crashed."

"*What?*" Finn cried.

"Our wives apparently spent the first part of Christmas Eve thinking we were dead." He shoved his phone into his pocket and opened his arms. Noelle came out of nowhere, and he caught her effortlessly. Over her head, he looked at me and Finn. "Good news, we're not. Merry Christmas."

Noelle half-laughed, half-sobbed.

I just kept hugging my husband, not letting go.

He came home to me.

Finn dragged me away into the formal sitting room for privacy. As we settled onto the chaise lounge, he put me on his lap and kissed me everywhere he could. My forehead. My cheeks. My lips. My chin. My hair. Everywhere he could reach, he kissed, taking away the tears and the pain with each one. After I settled down, he pulled back and cupped my cheeks, staring down at me with a tender smile and an intent look in his eyes that stole my breath away.

"Ginger..." He'd been calling me that since the day we met. Hearing it now was like music to my ears. "I'm so fucking sorry."

I nodded, closing my eyes and taking a deep breath. "I thought I lost you."

"I never wanted to scare you like that. I had no idea about that plane...I didn't have my phone on.

We got an earlier flight out, and we left in the middle of the night. I didn't tell you because I wanted to surprise you with my early arrival as part of a Christmas present."

I laughed, wiping my cheeks even though they were already dry. "Well, you surprised me, all right."

"Apparently," he said, grinning. "I'm sorry."

"There's nothing to be sorry for." I touched his chest, my hands trembling. He was real. He was here. He was solid. He was *safe*. I rested my forehead on his, breathing deep. "You came home to me."

"Of course I did," he whispered, his voice deep. "I always will, Ginger."

I nodded, closing my eyes.

He took the hint and crushed my mouth under his, his tongue expertly finding mine within seconds of me parting my lips. Someone cleared his throat, and we broke apart, laughing.

My dad stood there, looking sheepish. "Guess it's too late to say surprise?"

"Yeah, a little bit." I stood, still trembling but for a different reason. "I'm so happy to see you."

He looked surprised. "Really?"

"Apparently they thought we were dead," Finn said dryly.

"What?" Mom exclaimed from behind him. "Why?"

I laughed again, dragging Finn along with me by the hand. "It doesn't matter. You're not, and we're all here, together, safe and sound for Christmas."

Finn put his arm around me. "Of course we are, because we're family."

"Yes, we are," Dad said, pulling Mom close. We all smiled at one another like a sappy Hallmark movie, but I didn't care. All that mattered was that we were *here*. "Who wants some hot chocolate?"

Susan called out from the kitchen, "Me!"

"Already making it," Marie called out.

Finn laughed, and my parents followed their granddaughter's voice. We hung back a bit, hand in hand, and he looked down at me with the same heat in his eyes that had stolen my breath all those years ago, and continued to do so daily. "I love you, Ginger."

"I love you, too."

Leaning down, he pressed his mouth to my ear. "I can't wait to give you my present tonight."

Smirking, I winked at him. "Baby, you have no idea how lucky you're going to be. Santa is definitely visiting you."

His eyes widened. "Oh really?"

"*Really*."

He whistled through his teeth. "Is it time for him to come yet?"

"Soon, my love." I patted his arm. "Soon."

We headed into the kitchen, hand in hand, and I knew, in that moment, that I'd gotten a true Christmas miracle today. Even as I reveled in that fact, I thought of the people who didn't get so lucky on that plane, and their families. I made a mental note to find a way to help them. As he tightened his grip on mine, we walked into the warmth of our family (Riley, Noelle, Marie, Hernandez, Ben, my parents, Riley's parents) all huddled around the island with mugs in their hands, and I swore in the distance I heard bells ringing as Finn leaned down and kissed me under the mistletoe. "Merry Christmas, Ginger."

"Merry Christmas, my love."

Coming Next...

Coming home...

I've hated Ben Rollins ever since he broke my heart in high school. I've never fully recovered from it... even though I ran away as far as I could. Now I've returned home, fleeing something worse than I could have ever imagined. When our Captain partners us up together, I'm forced to realize that what I feel for him isn't hate at all. It's far worse.

Second chances...

Sarah's the one who got away. She never really explained her abrupt departure from my life, but to be honest, I no longer give a damn. What we'd once had was dead, and now I'm stuck with her at my side permanently, no matter how I feel about it. But when the truth comes out, and old secrets are unburied, being thrown together becomes so much more than a second chance...it becomes life or death.

And we have no intention of losing.

*Turn the page for an exciting look at the next **Out of Line** novel...*

On the Line

Sarah

The bloated, distorted features of the women's face were almost unrecognizable. The sun shone off the waters of the bay, casting a cheery glow upon the otherwise dismal scene. Birds sang in the distance, as a seagull sat on the hot sand staring at me, almost as if it knew that I felt as unqualified for this job as the man who had drove drunk and put this woman into the bay two nights ago.

Swallowing hard, I glanced at the picture in my hand, then back at the pale, swollen face that had already become a meal for some hungry fish. Though it was almost impossible to distinguish one feature from the next, I had no doubt as to who lay on the shore. "It's definitely Mary Hendricks."

Behind me, my male partner (who took the role of overbearing alpha male to a whole new level) shifted his weight onto the balls of his feet and scoffed. "Just like that?"

"Just like that," I said, tilting my head back to stare at the man who Captain had paired me with— more than likely, on purpose. Just to torture me. "Is there a problem, Rollins?"

"Yeah. I don't know how you did it in North Carolina, but in California? We usually wait for DNA or dental records to state who our victims are."

If I heard that phrase one more time, I was going to explode.

Ever since I'd come back to California, everyone had been throwing my abrupt departure for college in my face, as if it had been a bad thing to spread my wings and go elsewhere for a few years. Everyone might not know it, but I had a pretty good reason for doing so, and if anyone should know that reason...it was my partner. I'd had a damn good reason for flee- ing, and he knew it. Just like I had a damn good reason for coming back, after all this time.

"We did the same in North Carolina, but in this case?" I gestured at the victim's arm, pointing at the tattoo that said *Girl Power*. "I was with Mary when she got this tattoo, as well as the one below it." This time, I pointed at the tattoo that had *MLH* in fancy scrawl. "Which literally has her initials on it, so, yeah, I'm going to go ahead and say that this is Mary Hendricks."

Rollins flexed his jaw, staring down at me. "Still, no official word will be spread until we get the results back from forensics."

"Obviously," I said dryly, standing and swiping my free hand on my pencil skirt. I'd worn a light khaki colored one today, along with a checkered blouse. Every day I dressed, I spent way too long agonizing over what outfit would represent the woman I was now—strong, empowered, independent, responsible—as opposed to the girl I'd been— irresponsible, reckless, wild. The girl who had gotten her heart broken, and run away instead of facing the pain.

I wasn't that girl anymore.

Too bad no one else saw that.

Rollins gestured to CSI. "It's all yours."

"Thank you," I said, smiling at them.

None of them met my eyes. Typical.

Rollins started toward our waiting car without waiting for me. I followed him, studying his broad biceps and even broader arms. Once upon a time, I'd clung to those shoulders as he kissed me sweetly and told me he loved me, but that had been years ago, when I'd been another person. I wasn't that naive girl anymore, no matter what anyone else thought.

Sliding into the passenger seat, I opened the file I'd placed on hold and set the photos inside it, scribbling my thoughts down on the legal pad. As I wrote, I could feel Rollins' eyes on me.

"What?" I asked, not lifting my head.

"Why are you writing on paper? You'll just have to do it again later."

"Because I don't want to forget anything."

He started the car, shaking his head. "Okay."

I bit my tongue, refusing to rise to the bait. He'd been trying to get under my skin from the moment we'd been assigned as partners, and I wasn't about to let him succeed. "I remember things better when they're fresh in my mind."

"As I recall it, you never forget anything."

The sarcasm in his tone was impossible to miss. "I don't forget things that are important to me, no."

"So, your job isn't?" he immediately shot back.

"I didn't say that." I set the pen down and looked at him. "Don't put words in my mouth, Rollins."

He rolled his eyes at my use of his last name. In my opinion, just because we'd seen each other naked years ago didn't mean we needed to be on a first name basis on the job. Not to mention that had been a lifetime ago, and I'd never make that mistake again. "As I recall, you hate it when I do that, too."

"Then don't do it."

He shrugged. "What would be the fun in that?"

The sun gleamed through his driver's window, shining off his blond hair and almost blinding me. His jaw was hard, chiseled from stone, and he pressed his mouth into a tight line, like he usually did around me. His green eyes currently hid behind shades, but more than likely he'd narrowed them on the road. He wore a black suit with a white button up shirt and a sensible tie, like usual, and he gripped the wheel so tight his knuckles showed white.

It annoyed me how handsome he was, mostly because *he* annoyed *me* so much.

"Do you get off on picking on me?" I asked, unable to help myself.

So much for not rising to the bait.

His lips quirked into a smirk. "You know what gets me off."

"No, I don't."

The smirk widened. "Oh, right. That's one of the reasons we broke up—you never gave a damn about what I wanted out of life."

And just like that, I lost my cool. *Damn him.* "As I recall it, we broke up because you—" I cut myself off. Not doing this. Not fighting with my ex. *Nope.*

He slammed his breaks at the red light, swiveling to face me with flared nostrils. "Because I did *what*, Sarah?"

"Light's green," I said dryly, arching my brows, refusing to answer him.

He knew what he did. He just thought *I* didn't know.

He muttered a few choice words and stepped on the gas, his knuckles even tighter on the wheel now than they were before. It was a miracle it didn't break under pressure. "This is a horrible idea."

"What is?"

"Us, together again." He glanced at me out of the corner of his eye. "You need to ask for reassignment."

I rolled my eyes. "*You* can ask for reassignment."

"Why me?" he demanded.

"Why *me*?"

He pulled into the parking spot and slammed the car into park. "Because you're the one who waltzed back into town, thrusting yourself into my life uninvited, and—"

"I didn't thrust into anything of yours."

Yanking his keys out of the ignition, he pressed his lips together. "I know. I remember that, too."

I closed my eyes and counted to three. It did nothing to calm me down. "I swear to God, Rollins—"

"What?" He blinked at me innocently. "Too much?"

I glared at him, saying nothing.

"There's an easy fix to this."

Gripping the door handle, I unbuckled and hugged my file to my chest. My heart beat hard against it, faster than usual. Probably because of *him*, which only made me angrier. He took his shades off, and the force of his eyes locking on mine almost made me hold my breath. *Almost.*

"Oh yeah? And what's that?" I managed to ask.

"Do what you do best. Give up and walk away." With that, he took his own advice, opened his car door, and walked away.

If only it was as easy for me to do.

See How It All Started...
_____

**Read the first chapter of *Out of Line*
right now.**

Out of Line

Carrie

$\mathcal{I}$ leaned against the wall and surveyed the crowded room. All around me, people were in pursuit of the three majors of college: getting drunk, getting laid, and then getting even drunker. They were shouting in each other's ears to be heard over the deafening music, sucking on each other's body parts, or throwing up in a corner. The overachievers would do all three by the time the night ended.

It was freshman year at its finest—and I was the only freshman not fitting in.

But at least no one had been *paid* to hang out with me at this party. When I was twelve, my father had thrown me a huge birthday party. The turnout had been particularly surprising to me, considering the people who came were the same girls who told me what a loser I was while in school. Of course, as soon as my parents left the room to get cake, the girls had backed me in a corner and pulled at my hair and dress. They had told me that I was such a loser my father had to pay their parents to make them come. Susie had gotten an iPod. Mary received a phone. Chrissie—a pony.

I had gotten a cold, hard dose of reality.

A tall guy bumped into me, hauling me out of memory lane. His beer tipped and spilled all over my open-toed sandals. The cool liquid was almost a welcome change from the stifling hotness.

"Oh, shit. I'm sorry." He dropped to his knees and started patting at my feet with the closest object he could get his hands on. It looked like a shirt. "I wasn't watching where I was going."

I laughed and shook my head, dropping a hand on his shoulder. He felt a tiny bit sweaty, but who could blame him? It was freaking hot. "Don't worry about it. Seriously. It's fine."

"No, it's not." He lifted his head and his eyes went wide. "Oh, fuck. Do I know you?"

My smile slipped a little bit, but I forced it back into place. He wouldn't recognize me. I had been out of the public eye for well over a year, and I'd made sure to change my appearance quite a bit. I also had much longer hair, and my body finally grew into itself. My braces were gone, and I outgrew those god-awful bangs, too. I liked to think I didn't look anything like the gawky girl I'd once been.

Please, God.

"No, I don't think so. But don't worry about my feet. It's not a big deal. I was just leaving anyway."

He stood up. "Are you sure?"

"Positive." I smiled at him, hoping my sincerity showed. "Thank you, though."

He gave me one more smile and headed back toward the bar. I watched him go before I worked my way across the room. I needed to get out and breathe some fresh air. Somehow I even managed to make it through the crush without spilling my Coke. As I pushed through the door, the ocean breeze washed over me, immediately calming my pounding heart.

One thing I hadn't managed to change about myself in my big transformation: I still didn't do well in crowds. I never should have listened to my new roommate, Marie. I had only been at the University of California in San Diego for two days and had already been invited to four parties. I'd turned down all but this one. It wasn't because I was a prude or anything. I just didn't like the craziness that parties entailed.

After all, I had ultimately picked this campus because the occupational therapy program was excellent—not because of the parties. It also had the added bonus of being on the beach *and* as far away from my parents as I could possibly manage without leaving the country. They were great, and I loved them, but man, they liked to smother me.

The "hold me down kicking and screaming as I tried to break free" type of smothering. That was the last thing I needed at this point in my life. I needed to try to be on my own. To try to make my own place in the world. And for once I was really, truly on my own...outside of a raging party that I didn't belong in, hiding in dark shadows that hid only God knew what.

But still. Awesome.

I kicked off my sandals and trudged down the sandy hill to the dark beach, sinking my toes into the chilly sand. Probably not the best combination with the beer bath I had just taken, but whatever. My mom and dad had never let me walk barefoot in the sand. It was too unclean, and syringes might be buried deep down—plus other unmentionable items Mom blushed just thinking about. She couldn't even say the word *condom* for cripes sake.

I was convinced I must have been conceived via subliminal messaging or something. My parents were far too proper to do the down and nasty. Too proper to walk barefoot on a dark, scary beach. And I was supposed to be the same.

Grinning, I dug in even deeper, loving the way the sand felt between my toes. I scanned the shadows and found a bench a few feet away. When I sat down, I swung both of my bare feet in the air and let out a deep sigh. There was probably a homeless guy sleeping a few feet away from me in the darkness, but I didn't give a hoot. I was alone, in front of the ocean, listening to the waves crash on the sand.

For the first time since coming here, I felt at peace. Maybe I could fit in. There had to be some people here who were like me—a little bit dorky and a lot awkward. The door opened behind me, and the sound of heels clacking on the pavement interrupted my thoughts. "Carrie? Are you out here?"

"Yeah. Over here," I called out.

"Are you trying to get mugged?"

"No. Just trying to find a homeless guy to fall in love with," I replied, keeping my voice light. "So far, no one wants me."

"Whatever," Marie said, snorting. After a few moments, she stood in front of me, heels in hand and hands on hips. Marie frowned at me from behind a veil of perfectly arranged blonde hair, which blew in the ocean breeze. "You totally bailed on me."

I flinched. Yeah. I kind of had. "Sorry. In my defense, I did tell you parties aren't my thing."

"That's something girls say when they don't want to seem like sluts." Marie waved a hand and shoved her hair out of her face. Within seconds, it was back. "I didn't think you actually *meant* it meant it."

"Well, I did." I swung my legs some more, trying to distract myself from the righteous anger being thrown my way. "You can go back in. I just needed some air."

"Will you be back?"

"Maybe." I blew out a breath. "No."

Marie's light blue eyes pierced into me. "Are you going to be like this all year long? I like you and all, but you're kinda lame."

"I'll try not to be," I said as honestly as I possibly could. Because I *would* try to be sociable and outgoing and not so lame. I would probably fail. "But it will be a while till I'm there."

Marie rolled her eyes and fluffed her hair with her hand. "Well, hurry up. I'm not going to be lame with you as you struggle to adulthood."

"You don't *have* to do anything. Go back to the party." I shooed her away, a smile on my face. "I kind of want to be alone with my homeless boyfriend."

Marie eyed me, the hesitation clear in her eyes and the way she held her weight on one foot, the other slightly lifted. "Are you sure?"

"More positive than a proton."

"Oh my God. Never say that again."

I laughed. "Fine. Now go have fun."

"Okay." Marie hugged me tight, and her hair tickled my nose. "But next time, you stay whether or not you want to. Enough lameness."

I watched her go. We were complete opposites, but maybe it would make us great roommates. Marie might be the person to pull me out of my self-imposed shell, and I could make sure Marie studied as hard as she partied. It had the makings of a win-win situation.

Maybe.

Of course, it could be a complete and utter disaster too. But I was trying to be optimistic, thank you very much.

I leaned back against the park bench, letting out another sigh. I would sit here for another minute before I headed back to my room. Once I got there, I'd curl up with a good romance book with my current book boyfriend and pretend the real world didn't exist for a little while.

It would be the perfect Saturday night.

After a couple of seconds of pure relaxation, I

stiffened. Someone moved in the shadows. I almost missed it, but out of the corner of my eye I caught movement. Who was out here with me? If Dad were here, he'd be saying it was a druggie desperate for his next hit. He'd sic his private security team on whoever dared to walk near him. I used to go back to the spot and give whoever had been held back by my father's team some money. One of Dad's security officers would go with me.

But I wasn't my father, and I refused to jump to the worst conclusions. I stood up and crept toward the shadows, my heart in my throat and my legs feeling less than steady. My mind screamed at me to turn around and run home, but I ignored it.

"H-Hello?" I called out, but it sounded more like a croak than a word. I licked my lips and swallowed hard, taking another step toward the ocean. "Is anyone there?"

Nothing but the waves crashing. I hesitated. Someone was there. I knew it. "I know you're out there. You might as well come out. If you don't, I'll...I'll call the cops."

I held my breath, waiting to see if the hidden person would call my bluff and come out. After a few seconds, a shadowed form stepped forward. As the shadow grew closer, I realized it was a man. A guy who stood at least six feet tall and had muscles that I thought only existed in the romance books I read.

He had to be a couple years older than me, maybe a senior, and he had on a pair of cargo shorts and nothing else. Hot damn, he obviously worked out. A lot. He had short, curly brown hair, and he looked harmless enough. But those muscles...

Okay, when I goaded the guy out of hiding, I hadn't been expecting a freaking bodybuilder to walk out of the shadows. I backed up a step, biting down on my lower lip. "Who are you, and why are you hiding in the shadows?"

He had a black tattoo of some sort on his flexed bicep. Wait. Scratch that. He had tattoos pretty much from his elbows up and all across his shoulders and pecs. Hot. *Really* hot. This was the type of guy Dad kept me away from. He had bad boy written all over him. In numerous ways.

He rubbed the back of his neck and stepped closer, towering over me. "Who are you, and why are *you* hiding in shadows?"

I blinked and forced my eyes away from his ink. "I wasn't. I was sitting on the bench."

"Maybe I was too, before you came out." He grinned at me. "Maybe you stole my seat."

"Did I?"

"Maybe."

I shook my head and tried not to smile, but it was hard. For some reason, I liked this guy. "You like that word, don't you?" I held my hand up when he opened his mouth to answer. "Let me guess. Maybe?"

He laughed, loud and clear. I liked the sound of it. "Perhaps."

"Oh my God, he says something else." I held a hand to my forehead. "I might be imagining things."

"Hm. You *do* look a little flushed."

Probably because an off-the-radar hot guy was talking to me. Maybe even flirting? Crap. I had no idea. The last time a normal boy had flirted with me, Dad had his security team drag him out of the mall by both arms. I had no doubt this guy would get the same treatment if he ever crossed paths with Dad. "I do?"

He stepped closer and bent down, his eyes at level with mine. They were blue. Really, really blue, with little specks of darker blue around the pupil. People were always telling me that I had the prettiest blue eyes in the world. They were wrong. This guy did.

"Yep. Definitely flushed."

I cleared my throat and tucked my hair behind my ear. Until I remembered it was in a ponytail. Then I ended up kind of rubbing against my ear, trying to make it look like I'd *meant* to do that. And probably failing miserably. "I'm fine."

"I didn't say you weren't." He backed off and smoothed his brown hair, but it bounced right back into perfect disarray. He headed for the bench I had been sitting on and lowered himself onto it. "So, tell me. Why are you outside instead of partying inside?"

I followed him, scooted my shoes between us to maintain a safe distance apart, and then sat down on the edge of the bench. "Uh...I needed some fresh air. And this party is a little bit too crazy for my tastes. The frat boys are a little crazy too."

He nodded. "So, you new here?"

"Yeah. I'm a freshman." After smoothing the stupid skirt Marie had conned me into wearing, I looked at him. "Do you go here?"

"Yeah, I'm a senior." He cocked his head toward the house. "And I'm in that frat."

"Oh." I looked down at my lap. So I'd insulted his friends. Great. Just great. "I'm sure it's a lot of fun."

He grinned. "Even though they're crazy?"

"Uh, sure." I smiled back at him, but inwardly flinched. It was too late to tell him that the guys were perfectly normal. I was broken—not them. But I would look even more like an idiot than I already did if I told him I'd fled because of my own lameness. "Maybe I'll give it another chance."

He chuckled. "Not tonight, though, right?"

"Nope. Not tonight." I played with the hem of my skirt. "I'm all partied out. I drank too much."

He looked at my cup. "You better watch yourself. A lot of guys will take advantage of a girl who drank too much."

"But not you?"

His eyes darkened, but he looked away. "Not me."

It was a pity. I'd never been taken advantage of by anyone, but if I was going to be used, I'd prefer he be the one doing it. I kind of snort- giggled at the thought, earning a weird look from him.

Oh well.

He wasn't exactly the first person to shoot me that look. "Then I guess I'm in good company."

He shrugged. "You should go home and sleep it off."

"It's only eleven," I argued. I conveniently ignored the fact that I'd been planning on going home mere moments before. That had been before *him*. "Why would I go to bed already?"

He looked at me, running his gaze up and down my body. "You look like the type of girl who's used to playing by the rules. Good girls go to bed early."

I was, but I was also freaking sick of being that girl. All my life, Dad had neatly moved me around on his chessboard, a pawn to his own plans. I was done being a pawn. I wanted to be the queen of my own life from now on.

Leaning in, I caught his gaze. He stiffened, a light shining in his eyes I didn't fully comprehend. "Maybe I'm the type of girl who's sick of living by the rules and who's ready to have some fun."

About the Author

Jen McLaughlin is the *New York Times* and *USA TODAY* bestselling author of sexy books with Penguin Random House. Under her pen name, Diane Alberts, she is also a *USA TODAY* bestselling author of Contemporary Romance with Entangled Publishing. Her first release as Jen McLaughlin, *Out of Line*, hit the *New York Times*, *USA TODAY* and *Wall Street Journal* lists. She was mentioned in *Forbes* alongside E. L. James as one of the breakout independent authors to dominate the bestselling lists. She is represented by Louise Fury at The Bent Agency.

Though she lives in the mountains, she really wishes she was surrounded by a hot, sunny beach with crystal-clear water. She lives in Northeast Pennsylvania with her four kids, a husband, a schnauzer mutt, and four cats. Her goal is to write so many well-crafted romance books that even a non-romance reader will know her name.

Want to know what's coming next? Sign-up for Jen's newsletter.

Connect with Jen

www.jenmclaughlin.com
jenmclaughlin6@gmail.com